Text and illustrations copyright © 2021 by
Houghton Mifflin Harcourt Publishing Company

Text written by June Sobel
Illustrations created by Patrick Corrigan
Jacket and title page lettering created by José Bernabé

hmhbooks.com

The art was drawn with pencil and colored digitally.
The type was set in Bookman ITC and Schuss Hand ITC.

ISBN: 978-0-358-06366-7

Manufactured in China
SCP 10 9 8 7 6 5 4 3 2 1
4500818982

TOW TRUCK JOE
MAKES A SPLASH

June Sobel   *illustrated by* **Patrick Corrigan**

Houghton Mifflin Harcourt
Boston   New York

TO CLAIRE AND LEVI SEGALL—J.S.
TO GEORGE AND EDIE—P.C.

Summertime is full of fun,
and Tow Truck Joe is on the run.

Patch the Pup does her share,
helping Joe with each repair.

The ice cream truck's bell won't ring.
Joe and Patch will make it "DING!"

A camper's tire has a flat.
Joe can fix it just like that!

The beach bus stalls. It cannot go.
Patch inspects. Now Joe must tow.

Traffic grumbles on the street.
Cars and trucks overheat!

Hot trucks sputter. Hot cars beep.
On the road, they barely creep.

The tired tow truck needs a rest!
Patch the Pup knows what's best.

FREE ENTRY, JUST
TOOT'N'COME IN

10,000 BC

TAXI

"Let's cool off! Let's get wet!
Wash off all that dust and sweat!"

Driving to the Splash 'n' Shine,
the road is clogged. What a line.

STAY COOL
Let's Go Into Details

BRAKE DISC RECORDS

DON'T BLOW
A GASKET
THIS SUMMER
AC
50% OFF

HOT ROD'S
SUMMER
SMASH
"DRIVING
ME CRAZY"

☆101☆
DRIVE
TIME
TUNES

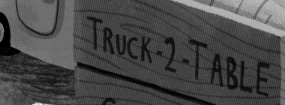

TRUCK-2-TABLE

GROCERIES

Sun blazes down on Tow Truck Joe.
But Patch sees why the traffic's slow.

At the car wash, someone's stuck.
It's Motor City's biggest truck.

"Oh my goodness!" Joe's pup squeals.
"This great, big truck has eighteen wheels!"

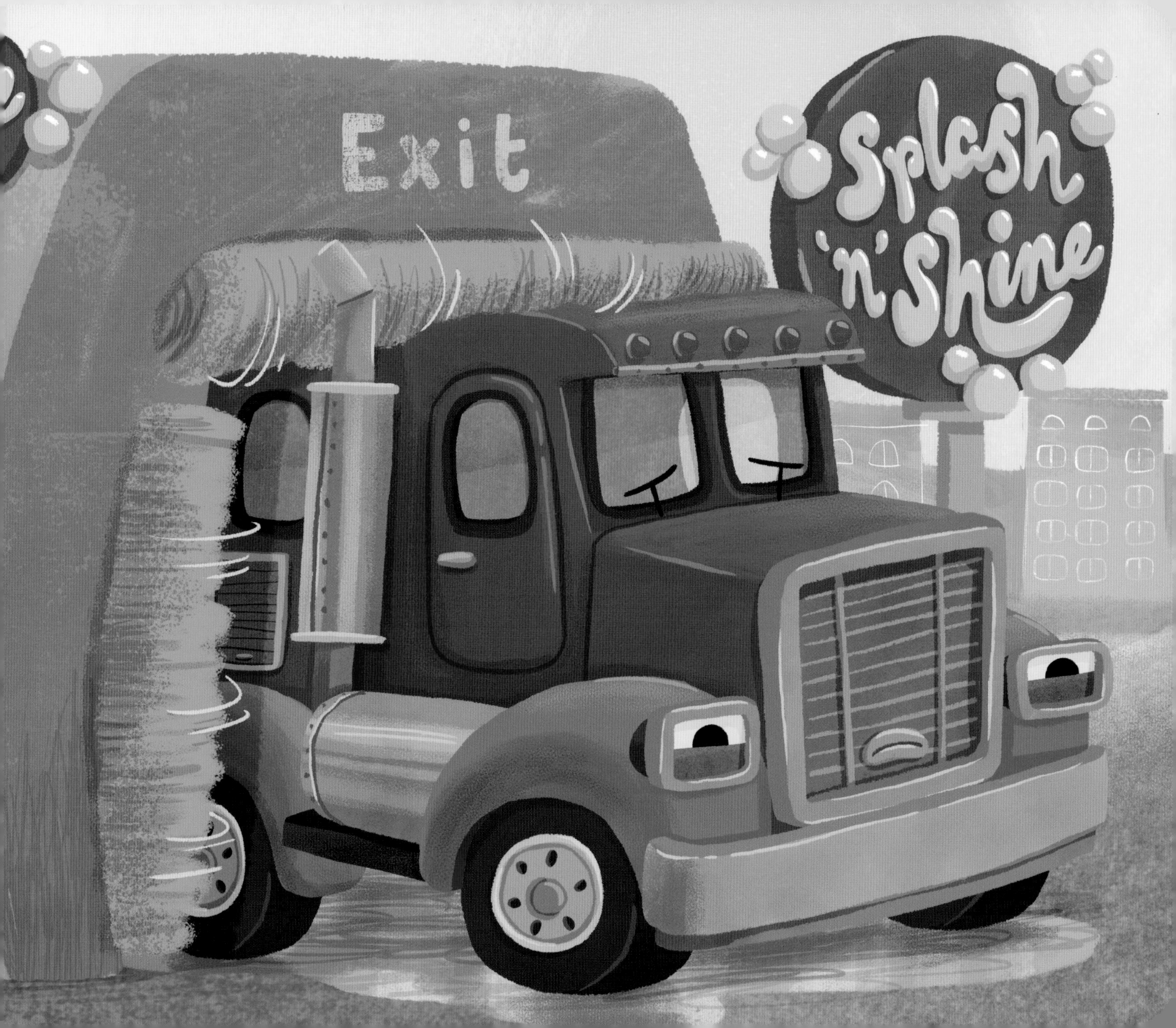
Exit
Splash
'n' Shine

Joe races to inspect the trouble
before the car wash turns to rubble.

He hitches up and tries to tow.
The semitruck will not go.

Patch the Pup lets out a yelp.
She sniffs around to try to help.

Soap sprayers turn up full blast.
The big truck's wheels move at last!

ONE for **ALL! ALL** for **ONE!**
We can fix it! Let's have fun!

Joe's tow pulls. His friends all push
the eighteen-wheeler in the tush.

GURGLE! BUBBLE! SPLASH! POP!

The semi lunges! Cannot stop!

Water gushes at full blast.
The giant truck moves at last!

Water spreads into a pool.
Cars and trucks are finally cool!

Joe skids on the slippery road,
soapy where the water flowed.

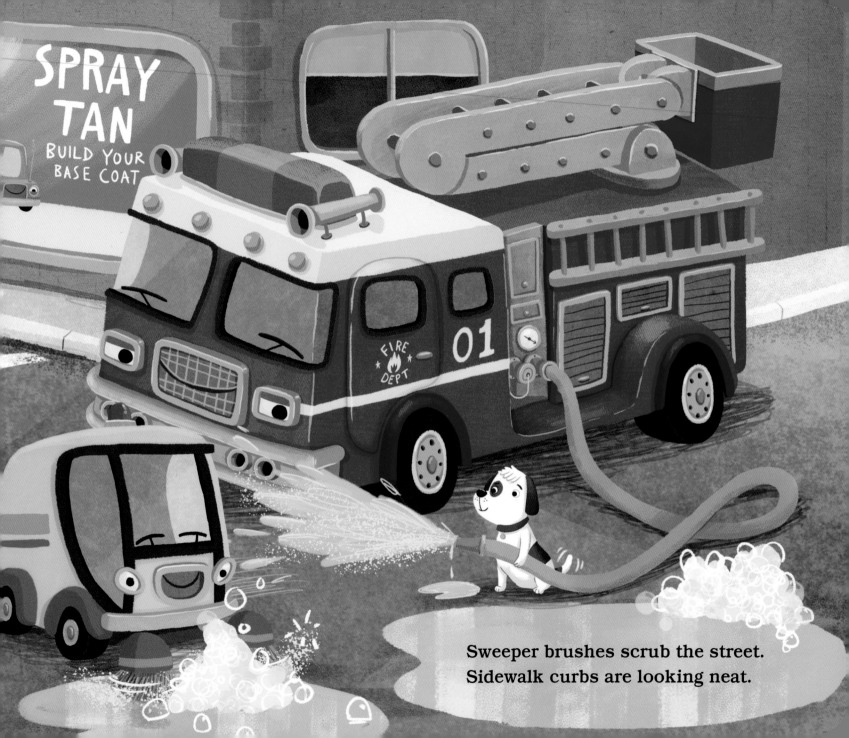

Sweeper brushes scrub the street.
Sidewalk curbs are looking neat.

All head back to Joe's garage.
Cars and trucks need a charge.

Parking underneath the trees,
they enjoy an evening breeze.

A summer day comes to an end
for Tow Truck Joe and his good friend.

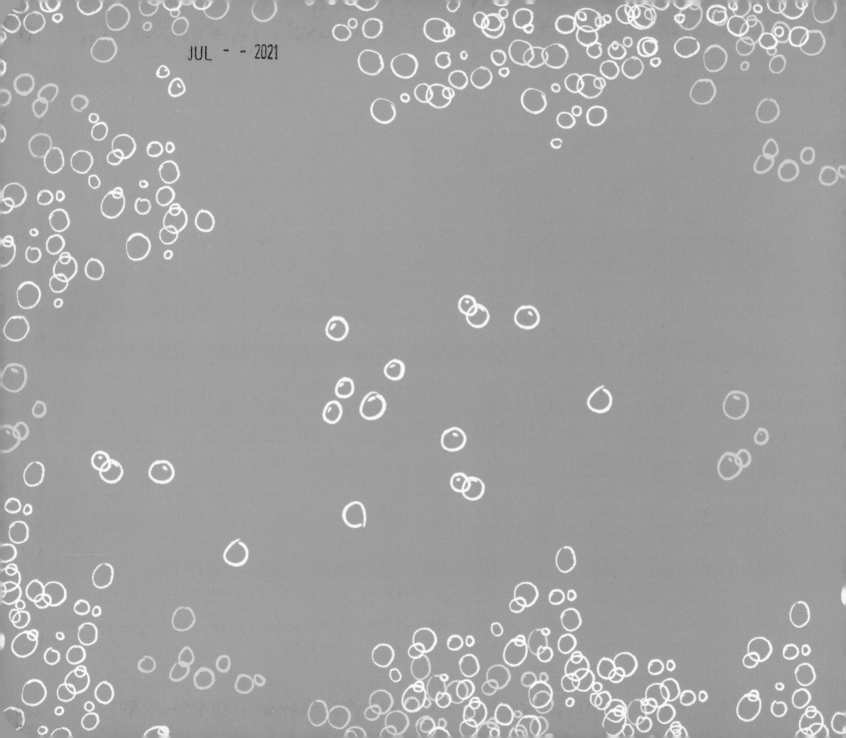